GIRLFRIEND'S DIRTY DILF

Straight to Gay First Time MM

Michael Levi

CONTENTS

CHAPTER 1

"You sure that you're happy with him?" Her father asked, making me feel more uncomfortable than I already was. We were in his house. My girlfriend was with me. She was the most beautiful, most striking woman in the world and I was so happy with her, which was the reason why I had to make sure everything was going to go smoothly here.

"Yes. I'm happy with Gregory," Victoria replied, putting her hand on my leg and then sliding it up, making me wonder if she was going to do what I wanted her to do, but which I was too uncomfortable to say with words.

Not to mention that we shouldn't do that in front of Glenn – at all. He was a big man, and there was no denying it. He wore a flimsy, skin-tight shirt that hung around his body, showing the contours and the outlines of his muscles. They bulged against the material, making me feel more awkward and uncomfortable than I should be, especially because for the last couple of months I had been doing my best in the local gym, only to find out that I would probably never grow as big as he was.

"Are you really sure about that?" He asked, squinting slightly and showing me that he was going to be a hardass to me again, just like all the times when we were together.

He always did this interrogation where he 'put me against the wall', making sure that I understood my place and that I could never upset Victoria. If I did, he would bury me alive.

"Yes. I really am. He's everything to me," she beamed, smiling broadly, showing me that she was going to support me through this difficult moment I was having with Glenn.

He was still only staring at me, his eyes scrutinizing me. In the meantime, my eyes couldn't stop checking every part of his body. There was something about it that drew me to him, to keep looking, and I didn't know what it was.

What I was saying to myself was that it was nothing more than admiration for him. After all, he was athletic, his body was toned, the muscles looked perfect, and he probably weighed twice my weight.

I really shouldn't be thinking this, but there was also something inexplicably alluring about the bulge between his legs. It was big and looked plump, too.

My throat was dry even though we hadn't been talking to each other for very long yet.

"If you say so," he shifted on the couch, widening the gap between his legs, and if I had thought before that he looked masculine, I misjudged it and was even more stunned now. He looked even more so, making me press my lips together, swallowing the lump that was in my throat. "But I still don't like this."

Victoria must have noticed that. She slid her hand further up and, this time, she was almost touching my bulge. She shouldn't do that, especially in front of Glenn. He wouldn't stand for something like that and I was certain he would beat me up. He would think that I was influencing Victoria to do this.

"Oh, but you don't really have to be like this," Victoria insisted, moving her hand off my leg, and I let out a cloud of relief after she did that. I had really thought that she was going to cup my bulge right in front of Glenn and, had she done that, I wouldn't have been able to hide the boner that was now beginning to show under my pants.

It was a good thing that today I was wearing jeans, I thought.

"I do have to be like this. You are my princess and I'm going to protect you from everything and everyone that can do harm to you."

"You don't need to worry about Gregory. He is really kind and always does everything I want."

He scoffed, standing up. I thought that he was done with me, but then he lifted his hand, beckoning me to him. I couldn't move my eyes away from his finger.

"Glenn?" I asked, my voice low and weak. My heart was in my throat and I had never sweated so much before in my life.

"You're coming with me. We two have something we need to discuss, in private."

"In private?" Victoria asked, her body language showing me that she was on the verge of throwing a tantrum. But then Glenn shifted his attention back to her, narrowing his eyes slightly again, and she fixed her attitude.

"Yes, little princess. In private with the man that wants to be with you for the rest of his life."

For the rest of my life? I asked myself. I didn't know anything about that. Victoria was nice and all, but I wasn't sure if I was ready to make such a commitment.

Victoria seemed puzzled, but then she just whirled around and stormed off. I followed Glenn to where he wanted, which was the backyard of his house.

When we were outside, he thrust his hand onto my right shoulder, slamming me against the wall. That hurt a lot and I winced, fearing that he was going to hit me and start to beat me up.

But he didn't know that. I had closed my eyes and then, slowly, I reopened them. He was looking at me as if he was studying my reaction.

"Mr. Williams, you really don't have to worry about me so much. I love Victoria and there is no one else that I would rather be with, I promise."

"I know."

I blinked twice. If he already knew that, then why was he doing this to me?

"Then... What are we doing here?"

"I want you to come with me tonight at 10 PM to Local's Diver.

It's a pub downtown, pretty classy and there's a huge sign hanging above the entrance. It's hard to miss. I want to have a drink with you and then we can finally start to talk about Victoria face-to-face and with our hearts. I want to know if you really are the right man for her."

I opened my mouth, ready to protest, but then I shut it in an instant. It was better not to poke the bear, I decided.

Just when I was beginning to wonder what he was going to do next, he pulled his hand off my shoulder and walked away from me, turning his head so that he was peeking over his shoulder at me.

And I decided to make sure that he had nothing to worry about by saying, "Yes, sir! I'm definitely going to be there."

"Good," he said without adding anything, stepping away from me and then back inside his house.

I exhaled in relief.

CHAPTER 2

So, here I was, my heart in my throat again. I was with Glenn and he was holding in his hand his whiskey. He turned it slowly, the liquid sloshing gently. My mind was so focused on that I was barely aware of the environment around me.

It was chatty, people joking here and there, behind me, some of the customers bumping into each other, almost starting fights because of that, and some music was also playing in the background.

What Glenn had said before about this place being classy turned out to be right. I would be enjoying it a lot more if I wasn't with him, though. His presence alone was enough to make me feel small and insignificant.

"I want you to know that Victoria is the most important person in the world to me. I want to make sure that you can give her everything she wants."

I was also drinking whiskey, though just like with everything else, I wasn't enjoying it as much as I should be. The bartender walked to the other side behind the bar, disappearing from my field of view. The fact that he wasn't in earshot made me shift on the stool where I was sitting, feeling even more uncomfortable than normal.

"It's like I said," I said, feeling like I was repeating myself. My eyes went up and down, checking every part of his body again. He wore the same shirt, his pants seeming to hang around his body. "I'm going to do everything for Victoria and I'll make her the happiest woman in the world."

"Good," he turned his head slowly and I couldn't stop checking the way that his muscles shifted, the veins popping out on his arms, the hair poking out over the collar of his shirt. He was so much manlier than me he made me feel like I was nothing. Even though I didn't want to admit it, my cock and balls shrunk in an instant, realizing that the difference between us was something that I would never be able to compensate for with anything.

A moment of silence ensued between us and I wondered what he was going to do. Without adding anything else, he tipped the whiskey over his mouth, swallowing everything.

"Come with me," he ordered and I wasn't able to open my mouth to ask him why he wanted to take me elsewhere. We had talked about Victoria and I had reassured him as many times as possible that I was going to do everything for her. So, this didn't make any sense at all.

But even that didn't appear to be enough.

He stood up from the stool and proceeded up the stairs, going to the second floor of the building. The pub was located downstairs on the ground floor. When I was already going up the stairs, I couldn't feel the intense odor of cheap cigarette smoke anymore, which was relieving.

I reached the second floor, finding myself in the hallway. I turned my head left and right and I found Glenn sneaking inside one of the rooms. The second floor of the building was a hotel and my ears could already pick up the voices and other sounds the guests were making here.

It was well soundproofed and I couldn't hear the music coming from downstairs anymore.

I was obedient. Glenn wanted me to go with him into that room and I was going to do just that. Without even thinking again about it, I opened the door, finding myself with him in the room.

I closed the door behind me and slowly turned around, my eyes bulging out. Glenn was naked. What the fuck?

I didn't even know that he could take off his clothes so quickly. When I had stepped inside the room, his shirt and pants were still covering his body, and I was certain of that. I wasn't making anything up!

But now he was naked and his hand was around his prick, stroking it gently and slowly. I was stunned where I was and couldn't move my body. I was frozen in place, realizing that this was the first time I was seeing another man naked.

And if I had thought before that his body was flawless, now I noticed that it was much more than that. My eyes couldn't stop moving left and right and up and down, checking every part of it. My mind couldn't stop wondering how he managed to mold his body to look like that. The contours, the outlines, and the shapes of his muscles were something to behold.

I felt my breath stopping in my throat, and for a moment it was like I couldn't breathe anymore.

My mouth opened and closed slowly several times in a row until I finally realized that I now looked weaker than ever before.

"Mr. Williams, what's going on?" I asked, my cock and my balls shrinking even more than before. My asshole clenched and unclenched, and I couldn't do anything about that. It was just my body responding to the overwhelming fear in my mind.

He smirked, showing me that he didn't have much patience for my lack of response and how weak I seemed to be.

"Come on, I know that you've been thinking about me this way ever since we first met. I know that you aren't entirely straight. The boner under your pants shows me that exactly, and I couldn't be surer about this than I am right now."

I still couldn't wrap my head around this, but there was no denying that part of me wanted it, too...

Mr. Williams turned me on like nothing or no one else could, and now I suddenly found myself wishing to fall to my knees in front of him.

CHAPTER 3

"Why are you looking so confused at me?" He asked, stepping toward me and, in a moment, I fell to my knees in front of him, my throat so dry.

"How did you know?" I asked and I felt like slapping myself for asking such a stupid question. He had already even answered it. I couldn't believe that I was going to suck off Victoria's dad.

He was such a DILF. I had always thought that about him, but I never thought that it would materialize in this manner and that it would be dictating the way that I was acting so slutty right now.

This was amazing and, at the same time, terrifying. I didn't know how it was going to shape our relationship from now on.

"I already explained that," he said, putting his hand behind my head and then guiding it down, making my lips touch his cockhead, and I knew that it was just a taste of what was to come.

"You really enjoy this, don't you? This whole time, you've always wanted to show that you were straight, that you were the right man for my princess, but it turns out that you are nothing more than another guy like me – I mean, that you like to experiment."

For a moment, I thought that he was going to call me a faggot, and it really surprised me that he didn't. He was keeping his hand behind my head and I knew that he wasn't going to move it anywhere. I guessed that this meant it was finally time for me to show my true colors, I thought.

I couldn't hide the excitement that I felt. It was in the

way that I kept on staring at his prick with wide eyes, looking dumbfounded.

"I'm just so happy that this is finally happening," I admitted. What else was I going to say? And after thinking that, I snuck my hand under my pants, feeling my erection. I started to stroke it gently and slowly, imagining this huge, menacing man giving me head even though I was certain it would never happen. He was not the kind of man that would ever do something like that – at least, not to someone so much smaller than him.

"I know," Glenn purred, taking a deep breath. "And I want you to know that this is the ultimate test. I want you to know that you can do everything for Victoria, including this if she wants it."

I looked up, finding his eyes, which were glaring down at me. I could feel the way he thought so little of me. Even though he wanted me to be the right person for Victoria, this wasn't about that. This was about him experimenting with another guy.

"I'm going to pass it, I promise you."

He chuckled. "We'll see about that." And without saying anything else, he lowered my head some more, forcing me to wrap my lips around his cockhead, and even though he was 'coercing' me to be doing this, I still found myself enjoying every second of it.

I just never thought that I was going to find myself naked with Glenn and much less that his prick was so big. It was bigger than mine… And well, I would never have thought differently. Of course Glenn was way bigger than me. It wasn't even a contest.

"Good. I want to make sure that this means as much to you as it means to me."

To be honest, it was difficult to say anything right now. It was the first time that I was giving a blowjob, and it was mesmerizing and overwhelming. I ran my tongue around his cockhead, making sure that I was mimicking my girlfriend as much as I could. I was hoping that my experience wasn't going to show and ruin the experience I was making him feel.

And as if to show me that he was in no way feeling that, he tilted his head backward, closing his eyes. The fact that he was truly enjoying this spurred me on, and I found myself wishing to bring him to his climax when the moment was right. Not before or after; only when I wanted to make it happen.

Except that it wasn't going to happen like that. When it came to how he wanted to control everything, Glenn couldn't change what made him the man he was. The moment when he realized that I seemed to be taking my time, he grabbed a handful of my hair, even though it was short, thrusting my head up and down several times in a row.

I soon found myself with his dick pounding against the back of my throat. My gag reflexes kicked in and I tried to move my head away from his prick, but that was easier said than done. In a moment, I was completely lost in the way that he wanted to abuse me as much as possible without hurting me – at least, not to the point where I was crying.

And Glenn was actually managing to do that. I never thought someone could.

In the meantime, my hand continued to shoot up and down on my prick, making it bigger and harder than it was. Breathing had become so difficult I was once again thinking that I was going to pass out, but it didn't happen – and I was relieved that I didn't.

Moments later, Glenn stopped shoving my head up and down. I looked up and found his mean eyes staring back at me as if he was planning on killing me right at this moment. And if he did that, it would be no surprise.

Except that the smirk on his face showed me something else. Glenn had other plans for me, and I couldn't wait to find out what they were.

CHAPTER 4

"Turn around slowly," Glenn commanded and the only thing I could do was obey exactly what he wanted. I moved away on my knees from him and couldn't help but feel some discomfort in the way that he was leering at me. He was always so overconfident that it could be slightly annoying, though I was of course going to make sure that it would never be mentioned.

"Nice. You are always obedient. It really looks like you might be the right guy for Victoria," he commented, stepping until he was behind me and I couldn't help but wonder what he wanted to do now.

After a moment of silence, he explained to me exactly what was going on in his mind. "You are still dressed. Take off your clothes and show me your body. I want to see the real you."

I couldn't believe that I was doing this. He wanted to see my body naked, and that was exactly what I was going to do. Without thinking twice about it, I started to take off my clothes slowly. I just didn't want him to think that I was rushing this, and I really wasn't.

I put my pants and shirt on the floor, my underwear on top of them. After doing that, I noticed him making his hand shoot faster up and down on his prick, showing me that he felt more turned on now that his eyes were feasting on my vulnerable body.

In the meantime, I just couldn't explain it. I couldn't explain anything. Here I was, a straight man who was now showing his ass to another guy. And the best thing about this was that he was enjoying every minute of it, too. Every fucking second.

Glenn was leering at me and I didn't have to be looking over my shoulder to know that.

"Good. Now that you are naked and I can finally see how you really look without your clothes, I can see why Victoria is so interested in you. She loves you, doesn't she?" He asked and I nodded.

I was so submissive. Everything Glenn wanted me to do, I was doing.

"Now, I want you to do something else. Do you think you can do it for me?" He asked.

Even though he was some feet away from me, I could still feel as if he was right over my shoulder with his lips almost touching the lobe of my right ear. That was how powerful his voice was. It exhaled manliness.

"Good. You really are doing everything I want, and I couldn't be happier about it."

Then, he didn't say anything, and I knew that he was checking me out carefully with his hungry eyes.

Just when I was wondering what else he was going to do and what he had meant he was going to ask me to do before, he ordered, "Lift up your butt. I want to see your ass. I want to see how pretty it is."

Lift my ass? For a moment, my mind couldn't quite process his request, but then it became obvious to me. Also, I couldn't stop thinking that I was doing everything so that I became bi. It was going to be difficult to look at my girlfriend in the face after everything that was happening here, and I wasn't ashamed of that.

I did what he asked of me. I lifted my ass so that it was pointed to his face, and he was overjoyed by what his eyes were feasting on. So much so that he didn't hold it back when he said, "Good lord. It's even better than my wife's."

I didn't know if I was supposed to feel flattered or if maybe he was trying to make me think less of myself. If he was trying to insult me, it wasn't working. My heart was speeding up, and all I wanted to do was to open my asshole as wide as it would go so that he could see it in all of its perfection and in full detail, too.

"Do you really think that?" I asked and I knew it was a mistake. I knew that because he was going to use it to his advantage, as usual. It was no surprise to me when he chuckled.

"Oh, Gregory. I think that and a lot more," he replied and then he went on his knees, standing right behind me. I could hear the friction sounds that his hand was making as he continued to stroke his member.

A thought crossed my mind that made me feel shivers down my spine. Was he thinking about impaling me with his shaft? I didn't know. I couldn't read his mind, but something deep in me was telling me that he was thinking that. It had to be his plan.

My body started to shiver, especially when he placed his hands on my ass, his fingers looking for my asshole and groping everything he could. Glenn was touching, exploring, and covering every part of my butt, and it was absolutely exhilarating and breathtaking.

I started to hyperventilate, but even that wasn't enough to stop me. Glenn went on, his finger tracing the crack of my ass, which was actually so much more than just a crack.

And then he stopped moving his finger when he was about to reach my asshole. I thought that Glenn was finally going to do it, that he was going to touch the rim of my orifice, but he had other plans.

Other plans that he didn't want to talk about right now, but which I knew he was going to employ anyway.

CHAPTER 5

"Gosh, do you use any kind of cream to keep your butt smooth and soft like this?" He asked and I didn't even know how to answer that. Was I supposed to? I didn't know, but at this moment, it also didn't matter.

His free hand went back to stroking his massive dick and I couldn't help but wonder when he would finally let me play with his balls. I was sure that they were massive – like two little globes that only a handful of lucky candidates could play with.

"I don't use or apply anything," I replied and I felt that I needed to answer his question truthfully. Anything else wouldn't do, I thought the moment when I felt his finger prodding and exploring my orifice - and that was something he was doing masterfully.

I moaned and groaned, and never before did I feel so happy and accomplished. Without saying anything else, Glenn held nothing back when he slid his finger into my orifice and leaned over me, putting his body on top of mine, and I could feel his muscles grazing over my back.

It was exhilarating. His sweat was glued to my skin.

I arched my back, putting my body more deeply against his.

"Are you really sure about that?" He asked and, this time, I had no idea what to answer. All I knew was that I wanted his cock inside of me right away, but I had no idea if he was going to do that – especially without protection.

I nodded and then he inserted another finger inside my anus, rubbing it, moving in it, turning in it, and grazing the inside of my entrance, making me feel shockwaves of pleasure through my entire body.

"Good. That was the answer I hoped for," Glenn admitted. Then, he added another finger inside of me, and I felt like I was running in a marathon. It was absolutely devastating, tiring, and breathing had become so difficult. I was hyperventilating again, and… And now I could feel his balls dabbing my ass every so often, and I shrieked in pain and pleasure, lust overflowing from me.

The way that Glenn was teasing me with a lot more than I thought he could do… I knew I could never think he couldn't do anything. Glenn was the kind of man that could always surprise me.

"What are you going to do now?" I asked and he didn't answer. Not immediately, anyway. I thought that he was going to, but he had other plans in mind.

His fingers were still inside of me, touching, exploring, turning me into his little plaything, and I was letting him do that and a lot more.

Seconds later, Glenn pulled them out and left me alone and wondering what he wanted to do now.

"You think that it's going to be so easy?" Without warning me, he stood up. So, this was how it was going to end? I didn't know, but I sure as hell hoped not.

I hoped that he was going to go back to standing behind me and that he would finally take my ass virginity. But that was, again, not his plan. His plan was actually something else – for now, at least. The part about claiming my ass virginity was more for the end of our little affair.

He headed over to the dresser in the room. He opened the top drawer and took something from inside it. I knew what it was. I had used it sometimes with Victoria, and that smell that came from it… It was quite characteristic, and shivers ran down my spine as I realized that he was going to do only one thing to me now.

Glenn was going to spread the lube in my anus. He was going to do that after he stretched me a little with his fingers.

"This is the final test," he announced, getting on his knees behind me again, and this time he inserted his fingers into my asshole one more time. I felt him spreading the lube inside of me, and I couldn't stop moaning and groaning, biting my bottom lip so that it didn't become too obvious that he was already making me feel some slight pain even though he wasn't doing anything special yet. "And if you get through it, you are going to be allowed to be with Victoria and I'll probably never pick on you again unless you upset her."

My body froze up slightly. That was a warning I would never be able to forget, thus I kept it in my mind. I was certain that I would always remember it every time that we met.

His fingers continued exploring the inside of my anus with the lube, making sure that he was spreading it on every inch of me down there. My body continued to sweat, and I knew that he was enjoying every second of what he was seeing.

A moment later, he finally pulled his fingers out. I felt immediately lonely and I hoped that he was already going to insert his prick inside of me.

Without saying anything else, Glenn closed the bottle of lube and put it on the floor by the side. I glanced to the left and found it, my mind registering it for the brief moment that I was allowed to see it. A moment later, he grabbed my ass with his hands, pulling me to him, and his dick started to prod and tease my asshole, and I knew that his intention was to keep making me wonder when he would finally take this to the next level.

"Ahhh, fuck. I'm enjoying this so much," he said before finally shoving his hips forward, punching through my orifice, and he did that without showing an ounce of mercy.

I had to grit my teeth and shut my eyes as tightly as possible so that I didn't start to scream loudly. And as that happened, he continued going through, further inside of me, and I felt that he was so big that he would touch my prostate – something that I never thought possible. But I also had never thought that anyone could be almost 10 inches long, too.

Minutes later, he was deep inside of me and grazing my

prostate. As he did that, he started to roll his hips after leaning over my body. His abs rubbed on my back and I felt his balls slapping against my ass. That meant that he was fully inside of me and that he couldn't see his dick anymore, something that made me proud of myself.

After tonight, we would never be the same to each other.

"I'm going to start to pound in and out of you faster, Greg. I hope that you are ready for it," he warned and I shot my eyes open, finding that unbelievable. Glenn meant that, this whole time, he wasn't at top speed? I just couldn't believe it.

Glenn held nothing back, pounding in and out of me. As if he was reading my mind, he increased his speed, fucking me beyond oblivion. I closed my eyes shut again and gritted my teeth, doing everything possible so that the searing pain he was shooting through my body wasn't going to make me pass out.

When he was done, I felt his seed spurting out, coating my insides, and it was warm and as viscous as I had thought. I started to groan and moan, letting out little squeals of pleasure.

When it came down to it, even though I didn't want to admit it, this was the best fuck of my life.

I was breathless and panting, and his fingers were still digging into the skin of my waist.

"I hope that you've learned your lesson. You can never upset my little princess and, if you ever do, you are going to get fucked so hard that every time you leave your house, you'll be looking over your shoulder, wondering if I'm going to show up, if I'm going to beat you up and punish you for being an asshole.

I didn't even know where that came from, but it worked. It put me in my place.

Glenn popped out of me, my asshole struggling to close again. It couldn't, I realized. My body was where it was and I couldn't move it. I couldn't even curl my fingers.

All I knew was that I would never feel so much pleasure again in my life – unless I wanted to submit myself to his desire again.

Glenn stood up and I was still where I was, with my ass pointed up to the ceiling. As if to show me that he couldn't care less about me, Glenn collected his saliva in his mouth and shot it onto my ass, his fingers coating me with it.

"I guess I should say that you passed your test. Congratulations! You can now be Victoria's boyfriend without having to worry so much that someone is going to kill you."

Then, I passed out.

I knew that our sex was going to take a huge toll on me, but I never thought that it was going to be so blazing.

Still, I couldn't erase the smile on my face. It was beautiful.

EPILOGUE

"What the hell happened to you, man?" My friend asked after sitting on the couch and realizing that my relationship with my girlfriend was over. To be honest, it was over the moment when I did everything Glenn wanted of me. I was weak. I was submissive. I was everything he wanted, and there was no denying that he got exactly what he wanted from me in the end.

As for the now… I was still living in his house.

"Robert, I think that I'm… bi," I replied and he looked at me with wide eyes, finding it all unbelievable.

"Come on, man. I know that you aren't like this. You are someone else. I look at you and don't recognize you anymore."

I shook my head. There was no point in continuing this conversation, especially because the man of the house had already come back from work. We heard his pickup truck pulling over in the driveway. He jumped out of the vehicle and, in a moment, was already in the doorway, leering at me. We knew exactly what he wanted.

"What the hell have you done to my friend?" Robert barked, raising his voice as he stood up in a blink. Seeing his reaction, I was alarmed. I thought that he was going to start a fight with Glenn and, considering the difference in size between the two men, I knew that he would lose badly, and the last thing I wanted to see today was my friend getting beaten up.

In light of that, I immediately settled my hand on his shoulder. I shook my head slowly and once and looked into his eyes, making sure that I was putting on my most serious expression.

"Don't do it, man. Just leave. This is what I want. I want to be with Glenn. I want to feel his big, hard cock pounding in my ass, and I know that he craves the same thing. He always says that I'm so much better than his wife, and to me, that is a reason to feel proud of myself."

He blinked twice, not understanding why I said that, but he didn't have to, anyway.

"I really don't understand what's going on, but... *fine.* I'm not going to insist on it if this is really what you want for yourself. I can see it in your eyes. You aren't lying to me and you aren't drugged as well. It's just a pity that things are happening this way."

He left me with Glenn and I was relieved that he finally left.

Even though I couldn't know this for sure, I felt that this was far from over. I felt that he was going to come back and was also going to learn something different about himself. I couldn't help but wonder what that was and when it was going to happen and if I was going to be involved in it.

I guessed I was going to see that soon.

The End

Thank you for reading this collection, and leave your review. Your feedback helps me immensely!

TEASER: CAUGHT LOOKING BY THE QUARTERBACK

Straight to Gay First Time Story (Bicurious Guys - 1)

I was just a college guy, like all the others. I was trying to fit in and look less like an idiot. Why did I have to stumble into the college's football team, though? I didn't know, but things were working out this way. More and more girls were beginning to show interest in me, even if it was only momentary... and I didn't think it was going to lead anywhere.

I sighed, closing the door by my side when I realized someone was there. Not too far from me, taking off his shirt and getting ready to put on his uniform. I supposed it was appreciation more than anything that was making me feel this way about the guy, even though I was 100% straight. Really, I was, and nothing was going to change that.

But nothing could have gotten me ready for what I was seeing. The guy was perfect. He was in his early twenties, so he was a little older than me, huge, with rippling muscles, and a beard still to be made. His hair was jet-black and his eyes the color of emerald. Every time he looked at me, he froze me with his gaze.

I couldn't stop thinking about him, even when he was in his room and wasn't doing anything more than playing on his computer. I wasn't going to say I was gay. I really wasn't, but I couldn't stop admiring him for being everything I wanted to become. Perhaps he could help me with working out at the gym, but then I didn't know if I'd be able to hide my boner... like it was happening now.

Not only I wasn't gay, but I also had to keep reminding myself that I wasn't a virgin, either. Not in the usual, more common sense of the word, at least. I had some experiences where it kind of happened with some girls... And I'd like to keep things at that.

Austin was now taking off his pants too, and I couldn't stop dissecting his perfect legs with my eyes. I couldn't help but imagine what it would be like to slide my hands over his muscles, feeling his hair, the curves that defined his legs, and smelling the scent of his crotch. Why was I thinking about those things of my team's leader?

I didn't know, but I was already feeling desperate and my boner was beginning to show. I came here with a common pair of jeans and it should be enough to keep it hidden. Austin could never find out that I had a huge turn-on for him, or else there would be trouble. This was a small college in the middle of nowhere, in a region known for being pretty homophobic. I didn't want to take the risk and then be forced to transfer to another university. It wasn't going to happen.

I took a deep breath and looked away quickly when he turned slightly. I didn't know if he was looking at me or not. We were in the dresser room and everything was pretty quiet here. Everything was so silent I could almost hear a pin dropping. I was a couple of feet away from Austin and I was pretty sure he wasn't thinking anything odd was happening here. After all, he had no reason to believe I was gay.

I took a deep breath in, looked back where he was, and I realized he was back to putting on his uniform. But he was still taking off his socks this time. He wasn't looking as imperious as before because he was seated now, his back turned to me.

But it wasn't that seeing him that way was making him look any less lust-inducing than he was. Even now, my body was frozen and I hadn't made much progress in terms of putting on my uniform. I needed to do that when my cock wasn't so hard. I should be punching myself that I was feeling those things for the guy that was always so willing to help everyone out, but it was just… impossible to control my feelings.

I heard the door opening and I knew that meant that things here were going to get more complicated. I could hear them talking out loud, cracking jokes, and laughing. It was the rest of the team. They were walking into the dressing room and were going to see that I was stealing glances at the quarterback…

SIMILAR BOOKS

GAY FOR BLUE COLLARS

1. Given to the Cop

2. Given to the Miner

3. Given to the Plumber

4. Given to the Firefighter

5. Given to the Mechanic

DIRTY FANTASIES

1. Filling in for the Bride

2. Filling in for the Wife

3. Filling in for the Girlfriend

ABOUT THE AUTHOR

Steamy MM stories, baby! Michael Levi can't go a day without sitting down and putting into words all the dirty scenes that sprout in his mind. His collection is diverse, but it's gay love only. And if you are looking for something free, check his mailing list. Warning: it can be extra spicy.

When Michael Levi isn't writing, he's chilling out by the lake close to his house. Nothing better than kicking back with a martini in his hand as he daydreams his next explicit scenes.